Playful Puppy

By Charlotte Hicks

LONDON, NEW YORK, MUNICH,
MELBOURNE, AND DELHI

DK LONDON
Series Editor Deborah Lock
Project Art Editor Hoa Luc
Producers, Pre-production
Francesca Wardell, Vikki Nousiainen
Illustrator Hoa Luc

Reading Consultant
Shirley Bickler

DK DELHI
Editor Nandini Gupta
Art Editor Shruti Soharia Singh
Assistant Art Editor Yamini Panwar
DTP Designers Anita Yadav, Vijay Kandwal
Picture Researcher Sumedha Chopra
Deputy Managing Editor Soma B. Chowdhury

First published in Great Britain by
Dorling Kindersley Limited
80 Strand, London, WC2R 0RL

The publisher would like to thank the following
for their kind permission to reproduce their photographs:
(Key: a-above; b-below/bottom; c-centre; f-far; l-left; r-right; t-top)
6 Dreamstime.com: Andylid (ca). **18 Alamy Images:** John Eccles (bc). **21 Fotolia:** Stefan
Andronache (br). **24 Dreamstime.com:** Leremy (cra, br). **25 Dreamstime.com:** Leremy (cra, cr).
28 Fotolia: Eric Isselee (cl); Viorel Sima (cr). **29 Fotolia:** Eric Isselee (cl). **33 Getty Images:** Gyro
Photography / Amanaimagesrf (tc). **36 Fotolia:** Willee Cole (cl); Eric Isselee (cb); Nikola
Spasenoski (bc). **39 Getty Images:** Image Source (br).
41 Dorling Kindersley: Richbourne Kennels (l).
43 Dreamstime.com: Blue67sign (tl); Excentro (br)
Jacket images: Front cover: Alamy Images: LJSphotography (l);
Dreamstime.com: Red2000 (br)
All other images © Dorling Kindersley
For further information see: www.dkimages.com

Discover more at
www.dk.com

Contents

Chapter 1
The New Puppy

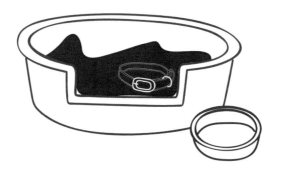

Holly had been waiting
for this day for a very long time.
She could not believe her dream
was about to come true.
Everything was ready.
There was only one thing left
to tick off on the list…
her new puppy!

Puppy Checklist

This is a checklist of things that are needed for looking after a puppy.

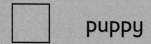 puppy

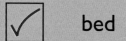 puppy food

bed

food bowl

water bowl

 6

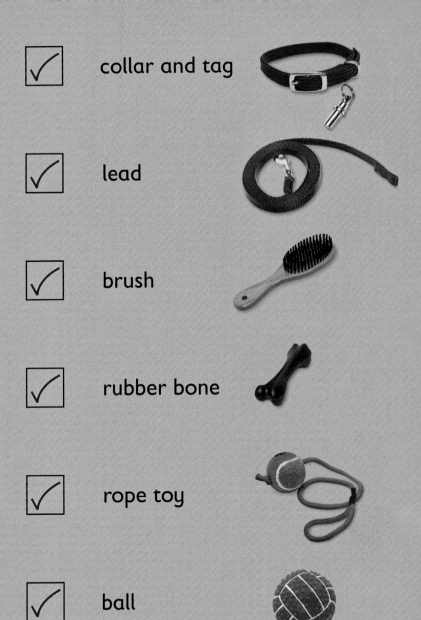

☑ collar and tag

☑ lead

☑ brush

☑ rubber bone

☑ rope toy

☑ ball

Holly's Mum and Dad
came into the living room.
Mum was carrying
a big, blue box.
Holly slowly opened the lid
and out jumped
her new best friend!
"I will call him Woody,"
said Holly.
"That is a good name,"
said Dad.

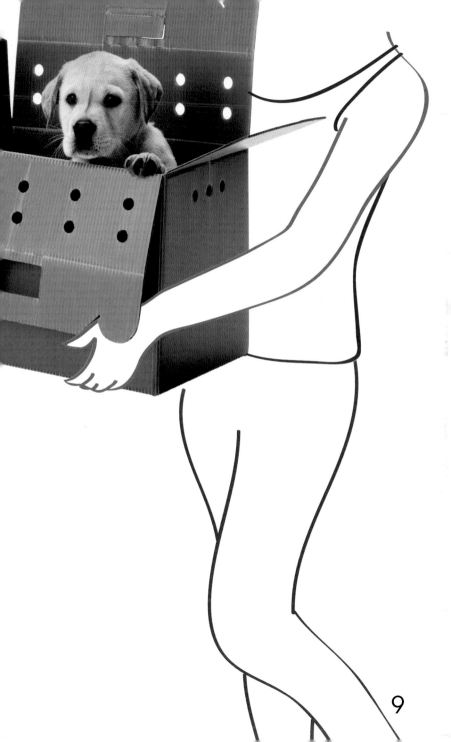

9

Woody saw Dad's shoe
on the floor.
Chew, chew, chew!
"Stop that, you playful puppy!"
said Dad.
Woody saw Mum's lunch
on the table.
Munch, munch, munch!
"Stop that, you playful puppy!"
called Mum.

Holly's big sister, Megan,
had left her woolly hat
on the floor.
Woody ran off with the hat
into the garden.
"That playful puppy
needs to be trained!"
cried Megan.

13

Parts of a Puppy

① ears

Dogs have an excellent sense of hearing. They can hear much better than us.

② eyes

Dogs can only see some colours. They see the world in shades of grey, yellow and blue.

③ nose

Dogs have a very good sense of smell. Their noses are wet, which helps them to smell scents.

④ mouth and tongue

Dogs sweat by panting. They also pant when they are nervous or excited.

⑤ tail

Dogs wag their tails
when they are happy.

⑤

⑥ paws

The front paws have five toes
and the back paws have
four toes.

15

Daily Timetable

Every day is very busy when you are looking after a puppy. It is important to look after a puppy well.

8.00 a.m.

breakfast-time

9.00 a.m.

walk in the woods

10.30 a.m.

morning nap

11.30 a.m.

play-time with toys

12.30 p.m.

lunch-time

1.00 p.m.

training in the garden

2.00 p.m.

afternoon nap

4.00 p.m.

walk in the park

5.30 p.m.

dinner-time

6.30 p.m.

brush and put to bed

Chapter 2
Dog Training

Holly went into the garden
to train Woody.

"Woody, sit!" said Holly.

"Woof, woof!" barked Woody.

He rolled on the grass and
wagged his tail.

"Woody, come!" called Holly,
but Woody had seen Buster,
the rabbit, hopping around
the garden.
Woody wanted to play with him.
He chased him round and round.

"Come here, you playful puppy!"
shouted Holly.

Suddenly Holly heard
a great big SPLASH!
Woody had jumped
into the pond.
He was swimming
with the fish!

"What am I going to do with you?"
asked Holly, laughing.
Holly needed to follow some
training tips.

Train your Dog to Sit

Here are some tips to show
how to train a puppy to sit.
You will need some small food treats.

1. Stand in front
of your puppy.

2. Show your puppy a treat, keeping
the food above his head.

3. Say the puppy's name
followed by
the command, "Sit."
Use a clear, firm voice.

4. Move the treat over the puppy's head. His eyes will follow and his bottom should go down onto the floor.

5. As the puppy sits, say, "Good sit" in a happy and excited voice.

6. Give the puppy the treat while stroking and praising him.

7. Repeat this many times.

Remember to be patient when training your puppy, and keep the sessions short.

Chapter 3
The Dog Show

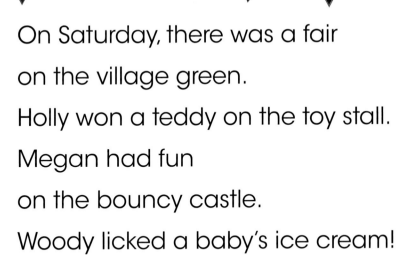

On Saturday, there was a fair
on the village green.
Holly won a teddy on the toy stall.
Megan had fun
on the bouncy castle.
Woody licked a baby's ice cream!

There was going to be
a dog show at the fair.
Everyone was very excited.

Dogs of all shapes and sizes
had come to the fair
with their owners.
There were lots of prizes to be won.

Fun Dog Show

Hillcroft Village Green
Saturday, 20th July

Come and join us.

Judging starts at 1.00 p.m. Lots of prizes to be won!

Could your dog be a winner?

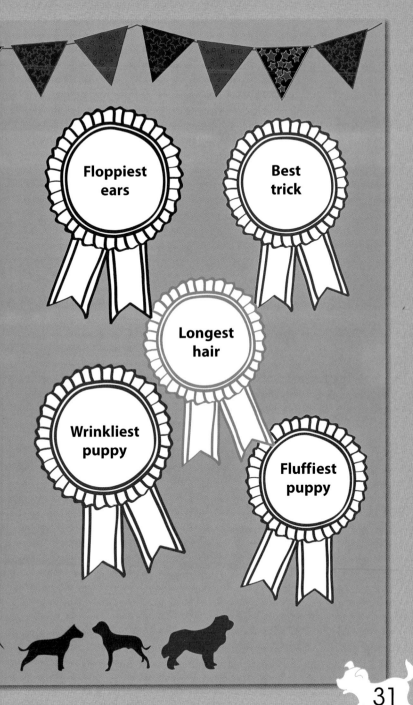

31

The judge came over

to look at Woody.

"Be a good boy," said Holly.

His tail began to wag.

Oh no!

Woody jumped up at the judge.

He left dirty paw prints

on her new dress.

The judge looked at

the other dogs.

Types of Dogs

Chihuahuas
are one of the smallest breeds of dog. They have big, round eyes and hairy tails. They are fast and lively.

Dalmatians
are large and strong. They have coats that are white with round, black spots.

English springer spaniels
are a kind and loving breed. They make an ideal family dog. They have lots of energy and need plenty of exercise.

German shepherds

are active and intelligent dogs. They like to learn and can be easy to train. They are often used for police work.

Labradors can be yellow, black or brown. They are very loyal and loving to their families. They can be trained as guide dogs for the blind.

Poodles are intelligent and can be easily trained. They need regular grooming and haircuts.

The prizes were given out
to the winning dogs.
They barked loudly and
wagged their tails.
People clapped and smiled.
Woody looked at Holly
with sad, brown eyes.
Holly stroked his soft,
floppy ears.

"I have one last prize to give out
to a special dog," said the judge.
Who could the winner be?
Everyone stood still.
All was quiet.
The judge said, "The first prize
for the most playful puppy
goes to…

… Woody!"

Holly jumped up and down in surprise!

Woody's tail began to wag.

He gave Holly a big, wet lick on her nose.

"Oh, Woody, you really are the most playful puppy!" laughed Holly.

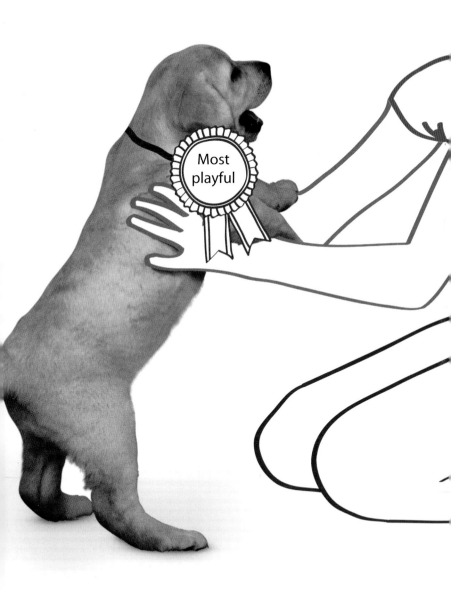

Most
playful

Congratulations!

This is to certify that

<u>Woody</u>

has been awarded 1st prize
for the

Most Playful Puppy

Hillcroft Village
Fun Dog Show

Judge B. Arking

43

Playful Puppy Quiz

1. What was the name of Holly's puppy?

2. What do you need to have to train a puppy to sit?

3. Where was the fun dog show?

4. What does a Dalmation's coat look like?

5. What was the name of the judge?

Answers on page 48.

Glossary

checklist list of things to be done

judge person who chooses
the winner

timetable chart to show the time
when something will happen

train step-by-step teaching to
do something new

treat small piece of
food to give to a puppy
when he has done well

village green outdoor space
that is covered in grass in a village

Guide for Parents

DK Reads is a three-level interactive reading adventure series for children, developing the habit of reading widely for both pleasure and information. These chapter books have an exciting main narrative interspersed with a range of reading genres to suit your child's reading ability, as required by the National Curriculum. Each book is designed to develop your child's reading skills, fluency, grammar awareness, and comprehension in order to build confidence and engagement when reading.

Ready for a *Beginning to Read* book
YOUR CHILD SHOULD

- be using phonics, including consonant blends, such as bl, gl and sm, to read unfamiliar words; and common word endings, such as plurals, ing, ed and ly.
- be using the storyline, illustrations and the grammar of a sentence to check and correct his/her own reading.
- be pausing briefly at commas, and for longer at full stops; and altering his/her expression to respond to question, exclamation and speech marks.

A VALUABLE AND SHARED READING EXPERIENCE

For many children, reading requires much effort but adult participation can make this both fun and easier. So here are a few tips on how to use this book with your child.

TIP 1 Check out the contents together before your child begins:

- read the text about the book on the back cover.
- read through and discuss the contents page together to heighten your child's interest and expectation.
- make use of unfamiliar or difficult words on the page in a brief discussion.
- chat about the non-fiction reading features used in the book, such as headings, captions, recipes, lists or charts.

TIP 2 Support your child as he/she reads the story pages:

- give the book to your child to read and turn the pages.

- where necessary, encourage your child to break a word into syllables, sound out each one and then flow the syllables together. Ask him/her to reread the sentence to check the meaning.

- when there's a question mark or an exclamation mark, encourage your child to vary his/her voice as he/she reads the sentence. Demonstrate how to do this if it is helpful.

TIP 3 Praise, share and chat:

- the factual pages tend to be more difficult than the story pages, and are designed to be shared with your child.

- ask questions about the text and the meaning of the words used. These help to develop comprehension skills and awareness of the language used.

A FEW ADDITIONAL TIPS

- Try and read together everyday. Little and often is best. These books are divided into manageable chapters for one reading session. However after 10 minutes, only keep going if your child wants to read on.

- Always encourage your child to have a go at reading difficult words by themselves. Praise any self-corrections, for example, "I like the way you sounded out that word and then changed the way you said it, to make sense."

- Read other books of different types to your child just for enjoyment and information.

Series consultant **Shirley Bickler** is a longtime advocate of carefully crafted, enthralling texts for young readers. Her LIFT initiative for infant teaching was the model for the National Literacy Strategy Literacy Hour, and she is co-author of *Book Bands for Guided Reading* published by Reading Recovery based at the Institute of Education.

Index

Answers to the Playful Puppy Quiz:

1. Woody; **2.** Food treats;

3. Hillcroft Village Green;

4. White with black spots; **5.** B. Arking.